I0556513

The Situationship Dilemma

Grace Wiley

Copyright © 2025 Grace Wiley

All rights reserved, printed in the United States of America. No part of this book may be used or reproduced in any manner whatsoever without written permission except in the case of brief quotations embodied in critical articles or reviews.

The Situationship Dilemma   1

Prologue   4

Chapter 1   8

  Sparks and Silence   8

Chapter 2   13

  Situationship Defined   13

Chapter 3   17

  Gray Zones & Late Nights   17

Chapter 4   21

  Emotional Bread Crumbs   21

Chapter 5   25

  The Other Woman   25

Chapter 6   30

  Zara's Ultimatum   30

Chapter 7   34

  Enter Malik   34

Chapter 8   39

  The Big Question   39

Chapter 9   43

  Clarity Comes in Silence   43

Chapter 10   47

  The Confrontation   47

Chapter 11   51

  Healing & Hope   51

Epilogue   53

Prologue

"We need to talk."

That was the message. Four words. No emoji. No punctuation. Just flat, clean, and cold.

Amara stared at the screen, her thumb hovering, not to reply, but to breathe. Those words weren't just a sentence. They were a signal. An omen. A rupture waiting to happen.

She was in the middle of folding laundry in her quiet apartment, surrounded by half-packed bags and the scent of her lavender candle. She had planned a weekend trip—alone this time. The kind of trip she usually invited Jayden on. But he'd gone radio silent for the past four days. Again.

Now this.

Her heart didn't race anymore at his name on her screen. It used to. Months ago, it fluttered. But lately, it just clenched—like it was bracing for a blow.

She didn't respond. Not immediately.

Instead, she dropped the phone on her couch and stood up, walking over to the window like it could offer a better answer than she had. Outside, the city was buzzing. Lights moved across the horizon. Couples walked below her, hand in hand, laughing. Real couples. Not... whatever she and Jayden were.

She knew what that message meant.They'd had "the talk" before.About exclusivity.About labels.About feelings.Each time, Jayden wriggled out of it with charm, clever words, or intimacy. And each time, she let him. Because a part of her—a part she hated—believed that maybe if she stayed, he'd choose her. Fully. Publicly. Proudly.

Amara closed her eyes. She could still remember the first time they met. The spark. The laughter. The night he walked her home in the rain without an umbrella, holding her like she was something precious. That night felt like a movie. But now, everything felt like a rerun.

She walked back to the couch, picked up the phone again, and read the message once more.

We need to talk.

A part of her wanted to type: *"About what?"* Another part of her wanted to say: *"Not again."* But the strongest part—the part that had finally learned to stop begging for crumbs—just locked the phone screen and whispered to herself:

"Maybe we do."

Flashback: The Beginning

It was a Friday night, and the city had that usual hum—the kind that clung to your skin like heat. Amara wasn't supposed to be out. She had sworn off social events for the rest of the month, tired of mingling with shallow men and answering the same "Why are you still single?" questions. But Zara had dragged her out with a promise: *"Just one hour. It's a gallery opening, not a nightclub. And who knows? You might meet someone worth knowing."*

She didn't meet someone worth knowing. She met Jayden Cole.

He wasn't loud. He didn't draw attention. In fact, he seemed like the kind of man who could disappear into a crowd and not mind. But somehow, he stood out. Tall. Calm. Sharp jawline softened by a scruffy beard. He had this quiet confidence, like he knew who he was and didn't need to prove it.

Amara noticed him before he noticed her. Or maybe he noticed her first—she couldn't tell anymore.

They both ended up staring at the same black-and-white portrait. A child's hand reaching through rusted iron bars. There was something haunting in the image. Amara tilted her head and said aloud, "Looks like loneliness."

Jayden replied beside her, "Looks like hope."

She turned, surprised. He smiled—not the kind of smile men used when trying too hard—but the kind that made you wonder what they were hiding.

They spoke for thirty minutes at that same spot, the conversation moving from photography to childhood memories to favorite books without effort. He didn't ask for her number immediately, and she appreciated that. He asked for her name. He asked what made her happy. He listened.

The next day, he sent a DM to her Instagram: *"Hope still looks good on you."*

And that was it.

What followed wasn't fireworks. It wasn't clear skies either. It was…
grey.

They went out—once, twice, then many times. He never said the word "date." He never introduced her to his friends. But he sent flowers on random Wednesdays. He texted *"Thinking of you"* at midnight. He showed up at her door with sushi and wine and stayed the night.

But then, he'd disappear for days.

No labels. No arguments. No promises.

Amara wasn't sure if it was magic or manipulation. She only knew that by the time she thought to ask what they were—she was already in too deep.

Chapter 1

Sparks and Silence

Amara meets Jayden at a friend's gallery event. The chemistry is instant.

The scent of paint, wine, and polished wood filled the air as Amara stepped into the gallery. High ceilings, soft jazz playing, and walls dressed in abstract emotion. Zara had already disappeared into a conversation by the drinks table, leaving Amara to wander on her own.

She wasn't dressed to impress. A sleek black dress, curls pinned up casually, and a pair of block heels that promised not to betray her ankles. She hadn't come to be noticed. She came to be polite—to show face, support Zara's friend, and slip out unnoticed before the awkward mingling began.

But then she saw him.

He was standing alone in front of a large canvas, arms folded, head tilted slightly. A quiet presence in a room full of people trying to be seen. He wore a dark olive shirt rolled at the sleeves, paired with black slacks and boots. There was no attempt at flash—just clean, simple confidence.

Amara found herself gravitating toward the painting he was observing, not because she was drawn to the art, but because she was drawn to his silence.

As she came to stand beside him, he didn't look at her right away.Instead, he spoke.

"It's loud, isn't it?"

She glanced at the painting. A mess of reds and burnt oranges clashing like fire against ash. It looked like chaos.

"Loud and angry," she replied. "Like someone screaming on canvas."

He smiled faintly. "Or maybe it's the artist's silence. The kind that's been held in too long and finally burst."

Amara turned to him. Their eyes met.

And there it was—the flicker.Not a spark that screamed lust, but something quieter. Slower. A pull.

They began to talk—about art, about the strange snacks being passed around, about how people pretended to understand paintings to sound cultured. He was funny in an unforced way. His voice was low, warm, and deliberate. He asked questions that didn't feel routine. He listened without glancing around the room. His name was Jayden.

Time slipped.

By the time Zara returned to find her, an hour had passed. She gave Amara a raised brow and a smirk, but didn't interrupt. Amara barely noticed. She was too busy watching Jayden talk about his love for street photography and how he once spent three hours on a rooftop to capture one perfect sunrise.

She didn't ask for his number. He didn't ask for hers.

But when she checked her Instagram that night, there was a new follower. A message followed shortly after:

"Next time, I'll bring a quieter painting. And better wine."

Amara smiled at her screen, thumb hesitating before she replied.

Whatever had begun that night wasn't loud. It was soft, steady, and slipping under her skin before she knew it.

Jayden is flirty but evasive about his past and relationship goals:

They started seeing each other more often after the gallery event. Quiet dinners. Rooftop drinks. Random bookstore visits that turned into conversations about childhood dreams. Jayden always had a way of making Amara feel like the only person in the room when he was present.

He was effortlessly flirty.Not the kind that relied on compliments or overused pickup lines. He had a way of making ordinary words sound like secrets shared between lovers.

"You wear calm like a crown," he once told her, brushing a curl from her cheek.

It disarmed her. Not just the words—but the way he said them, like he meant them without needing anything in return.

But when it came to talking about himself—his past, his pain, his plans—Jayden had a wall that looked like a window. You could see reflections, but never what was really inside.

Amara tried—gently at first.

One night, curled up together on her couch, she asked,

"Ever been in love?"

Jayden chuckled, the sound low and smooth.

"Isn't that a heavy question for a night like this?"

"Not if the wine's good," she teased.

"Let's just say... I've seen love. Felt something like it. But titles and labels... they tend to ruin things."

It wasn't a real answer. Just a dodge wrapped in charm.

Another time, she asked about his family.

"My family's... complicated," he said. "Some things are better left blurry."

He always redirected the conversation with a kiss, a laugh, or a change of subject. And somehow, she let it slide—again and again because the attention felt real. Because in the quiet between his words, he made her feel chosen.

But even in his presence, Amara sometimes felt alone. Like she was reaching out to hold something that shimmered, only to realize it was just smoke.

She told Zara once, half-laughing and half-hurting,

"He makes me feel like the sun—but only when he's in the mood to look at the sky."

Zara didn't laugh.

She just said,

"Then you better figure out what you are to him before your light burns out."

But Amara wasn't ready to ask. Because deep down, she feared the silence more than the uncertainty.

Chapter 2

Situationship Defined

*Three months in, Amara realizes they do everything couples do—
except call it a relationship.*

It had been three months.

Three months of late-night calls that lasted until one of them fell
asleep mid-sentence.Three months of weekend brunches, lazy
movie nights, and stolen kisses in parked cars. Three months of
inside jokes, playlists made for her, and Jayden's toothbrush now
casually resting beside hers.

But they had never talked.

Not once.

No mention of being exclusive reference to being in a relationship
"boyfriend," no "girlfriend." Just... this thing. This feeling. This
almost.

It was Zara who finally said the word out loud.

"You're in a situationship, babe."

Amara blinked. "No. We're just... taking things slow."

Zara raised a brow, sipping her iced coffee like it was truth serum.
"Slow? Or stuck?"

That question followed Amara home that night. It curled beside her
like a cold wind while Jayden lay beside her on the bed, scrolling
through a playlist he wanted to show her.

They had just finished eating Thai food—his treat. He'd even remembered her aversion to peanuts. Afterwards, they curled up like always, legs tangled, her head on his chest. She wanted to ask him what this was. What she was to him. But the warmth of the moment made her hesitate.

Why ruin it?

Still, the silence between titles was growing louder.

They acted like a couple. They touched like a couple. They shared memories, bodies, and even toothbrushes like a couple.

But when someone asked about Jayden, Amara stumbled.

"We're... seeing each other," she'd say, heart pounding because she didn't know what else to call it.

And Jayden—he never brought it up. He was affectionate, attentive, and even protective sometimes. But never intentional.

Amara started noticing the gaps.

The way he avoided introducing her when they ran into people he knew.The way his phone always seemed to be face-down.The way she didn't really know any of his friends.The way she wasn't sure if she was the only one he was doing all this with.

One night, lying beside him, she whispered,

"What are we doing?"

Jayden turned to her, brushing a knuckle across her cheek.

"We're enjoying each other, aren't we?"

She nodded, but something inside her sank.

It wasn't that she needed a ring or a big declaration. She just needed clarity. Security. Something to anchor the closeness. But instead, she was drifting, attached but unclaimed.

That night, as Jayden slept peacefully beside her, Amara stared at the ceiling and finally named it for what it was:

A situationship.

And once you name a thing, you can't unknow it.

Zara warns Amara, but Amara insists it's just "complicated."

Later that week, Amara and Zara sat across from each other at their usual spot—a quiet rooftop café with twinkling lights and a soft city breeze. Zara had that look in her eye—the one Amara had seen many times before. Concern, wrapped in sarcasm, ready to be served cold.

"So… you still playing girlfriend without the title?" Zara asked, poking at her fries.

Amara sighed. She stirred her drink with the straw, avoiding eye contact.

"It's not like that."

Zara leaned in.

"Then what is it like? 'Cause from where I'm sitting, it sounds like you're giving full-course energy to someone serving you crumbs."

Amara forced a smile. "It's just… complicated."

Zara's eyebrow shot up.

"That's code for 'I'm settling, but I don't want to say it out loud.'"

Amara chuckled under her breath, but it was defensive.

"Jayden isn't a bad guy. He's just... different. Guarded. He's been through things, and I get that. It takes time."

"And how much time exactly? A year? Two? Until he finds someone else and tells you he was 'never ready'?"

Amara looked down at her napkin, folding the corner again and again. She hated how Zara could see right through her.

"I don't want to pressure him," she said quietly.

"But what about pressuring yourself?" Zara replied. "You deserve to know what you are to someone. You're not a placeholder, Amara."

Amara didn't answer. Not because she didn't have anything to say, but because deep down, she knew Zara was right.

Still, the word *"complicated"* felt safer than the truth. Safer than saying: *"I'm afraid that if I ask for more, I'll lose everything."*

So she shrugged and said again,

"It's complicated."

Zara leaned back, exhaling slowly.

"Just make sure you're not the only one confused."

Chapter 3

Grey Zones & Late Nights

It started slowly. Little things. Quiet things.

Jayden began staying the night more often. He knew how she liked her tea—ginger, no sugar. He remembered the brand of lotion she used and teased her about the way she always folded her socks before bed. They spent entire weekends together, tangled in sheets and laughter, ordering takeout and binge-watching crime thrillers like it was a tradition.

And in those moments, it felt like something real. Something full. Something that could turn into forever.

But then... he'd vanish.

A text left unread.A call unanswered.A full twenty-four hours, sometimes two or three, with no explanation.

At first, Amara made excuses for him.

"He's probably busy with a shoot."Maybe his battery died."He's not the texting type."

But the knot in her chest tightened each time.

Then, like clockwork, he'd return—with flowers, or a long, slow kiss, or a story about a last-minute gig that "got crazy." And just like that, he'd melt back into her world like he never left.

He'd show up at her door with that lazy grin and say something like:

"Missed this face."

And the anger would drain. The loneliness would retreat. She'd let him in. Again.

One night, after four full days of silence, he arrived with her favourite jollof rice from that one Ghanaian place across town and a new photo book he said reminded him of her. They didn't talk about the silence. They just... picked up where they left off.

And in the soft hours between 1 a.m. and 3 a.m., when the lights were off and her head rested on his chest, Amara would whisper questions into the dark.

But never aloud.

"Do you miss me when you're gone?" "Am I the only one?" "Why don't you say what this is?"

The questions floated in her chest like unspoken vows, and the answers never came. Just the rhythm of his breathing.And the ache of a love not fully named.

One evening, while lying in bed after he'd drifted off, Amara stared at the ceiling and realized something:

They had intimacy. They had a routine. They had comfort.

But they didn't have clarity.

Jayden's presence was a warm flame. But his absences? They were ice water to her soul.

And somehow, she kept choosing the fire, even though it flickered without warning.

Amara struggles to define what they are but avoids pushing too hard:

Some nights, Amara would open their chat, scroll all the way back to the first message—the one after the gallery event—and reread their early conversations. Back then, everything felt light. Uncomplicated. New.

Now, it felt like a puzzle missing one piece.

She wanted to ask him. She *needed* to ask him: *"What are we, Jayden?"*

But every time the words gathered on her tongue, they melted under the weight of fear.

What if asking made it awkward?What if asking broke the rhythm they had?What if the answer wasn't what she wanted to hear?

So instead of asking, she smiled when he showed up late and made excuses when he didn't call. She told herself she was patient, understanding, and mature. That love—whatever this was—needed space to breathe.

But deep down, she was just scared.

Scared that if she asked for more, he'd give her less.Scared that defining it would destroy it.Scared that the truth would end the fantasy she clung to so tightly.

Once, while they were eating ice cream on the hood of his car, watching the city lights blink in the distance, she almost did it. She turned to him and said,

"Jayden… do you ever think about… where this is going?"

He didn't look at her. Just kept his gaze on the skyline.

"I try not to think too far ahead," he said casually. "I just like being here. With you. Right now."

And that was it.

A beautiful, meaningless answer.Wrapped in charm. Delivered with just enough tenderness to make her second-guess her discomfort.

So she nodded, smiled, and changed the subject. Because maybe *now* was better than *never.*

But later that night, lying in her bed alone while his scent lingered on her pillow, Amara whispered to herself:

"I don't know what we are. And I'm starting to think… he likes it that way."

Chapter 4

Emotional Bread Crumbs

They were sitting on the floor of Jayden's apartment, surrounded by half-eaten Chinese food and records playing softly in the background. The rain tapped the windows like gentle fingers, and the dim lighting made everything feel softer, closer, more intimate. Amara had just told him a story about her teenage years—how her mother once caught her sneaking out to a party and made her scrub the entire house the next day as punishment. Jayden laughed, but then, something in his eyes shifted. The joy dimmed. His gaze wandered to the window.

"I don't have stories like that," he said quietly.

Amara tilted her head, curious. "Like what?"

"Stories about being caught. Or grounded. Or even... cared about like that."

She sat up straighter, sensing the change in energy. He was still looking away, his voice low and steady.

"My mom left when I was ten. Said she was going to the store and just... didn't come back. My dad was around, but not really. He worked night shifts, drank during the day. I figured things out on my own."

It wasn't a dramatic confession. There were no tears. No big pause for effect. It came out like fact—plain and flat—but it hit Amara like thunder.

Jayden pulled his knees closer, fingers absently tracing the edge of a takeout box.

"People always think I'm closed off. Like I'm hiding something. I'm not. I just... never learned how to let people stay."

Amara's heart tightened.

For the first time, she saw the boy behind the man—the little boy abandoned, unchosen, and left to piece himself together without instructions. The silence between them felt heavier than ever.

She crawled closer, gently placing her hand on his.

"I'm not trying to fix you," she said softly. "But I see you."

He looked at her then, really looked. And there was something raw in his eyes. Something broken. Something that begged not to be judged.

He leaned in and kissed her, slow, searching, vulnerable. And Amara felt it: the wall between them cracking.

That night, they didn't make love. They held each other. Quietly. Tightly. Like two people clinging to something fragile and fleeting.

In the days that followed, Jayden was more attentive. He texted her good morning. Called her in the afternoon to hear her voice. Stayed over more often, lingered longer. And Amara, desperate to believe, took it as progress. As proof that he was finally letting her in.

But looking back, she would realize—it was just another breadcrumb. A small dose of vulnerability.Enough to keep her close. But never close enough.

She feels she's helping him heal, and that makes her stay.

Amara couldn't stop thinking about that night.

The way Jayden's voice softened when he spoke about his mother.

The way his eyes clouded when he admitted he never learned how to let people stay. She had seen something in him—something wounded, something beautiful, something worth saving.

For days after, his vulnerability echoed in her mind like a secret only she was allowed to hold.

And with every small gesture—his fingers laced with hers while walking down the street, the kiss he placed on her forehead before sleep, the quiet thanks he whispered when she brought him food without asking—Amara felt needed. Chosen. Essential.

He's just scared, she told herself. *He's healing. And maybe… I'm part of that healing.*

That thought made her stay.

Even when he disappeared again for two days with no explanation.Even when she found herself replaying voice notes just to hear him speak.Even when her friends rolled their eyes and said, "Girl, come on."

Amara believed she was the exception. The one who could break through. The one who could love him enough to erase what others had done to him.

Because what they had felt real, at least in fragments.

She told herself that love wasn't always loud or clear. Sometimes it was quiet. Complicated. Damaged.

And she could live with that. She *had* to.

Because believing she was helping him become whole made it easier to ignore the parts of herself breaking in the process.

Chapter 5

The Other Woman

It was supposed to be a normal evening.

Amara had picked up Jayden's favourite Thai takeout on her way over, humming along to an old love song on the radio, her heart surprisingly light. Things had been better lately—he'd been more present, more affectionate. She thought maybe they were finally turning a corner.

The door was unlocked when she arrived. He'd texted her earlier: *"Come in whenever. I'm just editing photos."*

Inside, the apartment smelled like coffee and cologne. Familiar. Warm. His laptop was open on the kitchen counter, a slideshow of black-and-white portraits playing across the screen.

She walked toward the couch to drop her bag when something caught her eye—barely visible, half-tucked beneath the throw pillow.

A lipstick.

Deep red.Not her shade.Not her brand.

Amara stared at it for a moment, her breath catching like she'd stepped into a trap. Her hand hovered before she picked it up, slowly, like it might burn her fingers.

Jayden walked in from the bedroom, shirtless, towel slung over his shoulder.

"Hey," he said with that easy smile. "You beat me to it."

Amara didn't respond. She simply held up the lipstick.

The smile on Jayden's face faltered, just slightly.

"That?" he said, scratching the back of his neck. "It's not what you think."

"Then what is it?" Her voice was steady, but low.

He walked over, glanced at the lipstick like it were nothing.

"It's a friend's. She was here last week—dropped it by mistake when we were working on a shoot. I meant to give it back."

"A friend," Amara echoed.

Jayden nodded casually. Too casually.

"She's just someone I've worked with before. It's not a big deal."

Amara felt the heat rise in her chest, but not from rage—yet. It was confusion, Disbelief. The sharp sting of reality tapped her on the shoulder.

"Was she here… when I called and you didn't answer?" she asked, eyes locked on his.

Jayden shook his head. "Come on, Amara. Don't do that."

"Don't know *what*?"

"Don't read into things. You know I'm not like that."

He said it with that same calm, that same quiet deflection that always made her second-guess herself.

But this time, the silence after his explanation didn't soothe her. It suffocated her.

Amara placed the lipstick on the table and stepped back like it had betrayed her.

"You say I'm the one who's reading into things, but what exactly *am* I supposed to read? You disappear, reappear, drop crumbs of affection, and I'm supposed to smile and hold on to them like they mean everything."

Jayden's expression shifted—defensive now, like a child caught in a half-truth.

"I told you—I'm not good at this label thing."

"No," Amara whispered. "You're just good at keeping things blurry."

For the first time, she didn't wait for a follow-up excuse. She grabbed her bag, left the takeout on the table, and walked toward the door.

Jayden called after her.

"Amara, don't leave like this."

But she didn't turn around.

Because suddenly, it didn't feel like she was walking out of his apartment.

It felt like she was walking out of the illusion she had built around him.

Amara leaves but later returns after a "deep talk."

Amara didn't sleep that night.

She tossed beneath her covers, replaying the scene over and over— the lipstick, the shrug in Jayden's voice, the way he called after her like she was being unreasonable. Her chest felt hollow, like something had finally snapped loose inside her.

Zara had called to check on her, and Amara had kept her answers short.

"I'm okay," she said. "Just thinking."

But the truth was, she wasn't okay.

She was exhausted. From wondering. From guessing. From giving him the benefit of the doubt one too many times. And yet, underneath the ache was another feeling—one she didn't want to name.

Hope.

Because, despite everything, a part of her still wanted him to fight for her. To show up. To *care enough.*

And Jayden did. Two days later.

He texted first: *"I owe you a real conversation."* Then: *"Come over. No games. Just truth."*

Against her better judgment—and Zara's—Amara went.

He had cleaned the apartment. Lit candles. Played the soft music he knew she liked. But more than that, he looked different—tired, serious, unguarded.

They sat on opposite ends of the couch. No touching. No teasing. Jayden sighed before he spoke.

"You're right. I blur lines. I've always done it because it's easier than being vulnerable. And because I don't want to hurt anyone. But I realize now that I'm hurting *you* by not being honest."

Amara didn't interrupt.

"The lipstick... it really was from a friend. Nothing happened. But I get why it didn't look good. And I'm sorry. I should've made you feel safer. I should've been clearer."

There was a pause—one of those moments where the silence held more weight than words ever could.

"So what now?" Amara finally asked.

Jayden leaned forward.

"I don't want to lose you, Amara. I don't know how to do this perfectly. But I want to try. If you'll let me."

It wasn't a promise. It wasn't a label. But it was more than she'd ever gotten.

And because her heart still ached for the version of him that held her like she was home... she stayed.

They kissed softly that night—no passion, just quiet need. And for a brief moment, she let herself believe that maybe this time... it would be different.

Maybe this time... he meant it.

Chapter 6

Zara's Ultimatum

Amara hadn't planned to tell Zara she went back.

But best friends have a sixth sense. And Zara? She didn't miss much.

They were at their usual café again—same rooftop, same city breeze, but this time Zara's eyes weren't filled with playful sarcasm. They were heavy. Serious.

"You went back to him, didn't you?" she asked, stirring her iced latte like it had offended her.

Amara hesitated. Then nodded.

Zara leaned back in her chair, lips pressed together. She didn't say anything at first. Just stared at her like she was trying to figure out which version of Amara was sitting in front of her.

"What did he say?" she asked eventually.

"That he wants to try," Amara said quietly. "That he doesn't want to lose me."

"And you believed him?"

Amara opened her mouth, then closed it. She hated how unsure she sounded even to herself.

Zara leaned in.

"You're in love with a man who won't even call you his girlfriend."

The words hit Amara like cold water. She looked away, out toward the skyline, hoping her silence would say something wiser than she could.

"You make excuses for him, Amara," Zara continued. "Every time he disappears, every time he dodges a question, every time he keeps you in the grey. You bend yourself to fit his comfort while he refuses to give you clarity."

"It's not that simple," Amara whispered.

"It's exactly that simple," Zara snapped. "If a man wants you, you'll know. If he doesn't, you'll be confused. And you've been confused since day one."

Amara's eyes stung, but she blinked the tears away.

"He's broken, Z. I see his wounds. I *get* him."

Zara softened, but only slightly.

"I know you do. That's what makes you special. But love isn't about fixing someone. It's about choosing each other fully. Consistently. And he hasn't chosen you, Amara. Not really."

Silence settled between them, heavier than the city air.

"You deserve more than breadcrumbs," Zara added gently. "You deserve a table. A chair with your name on it. Not just... being someone's emotional halfway house."

Amara didn't respond. She couldn't. Her heart was in a thousand pieces, but none of them knew how to let go.

"Just promise me one thing," Zara said finally. "Don't lose yourself trying to make him whole."

Amara nodded slowly, but even as she promised, she knew the truth:

She was already unravelling.

Amara begins journaling her emotions:

That night, after Zara's words had settled deep in her chest like stones, Amara found herself sitting on her bedroom floor with an old, half-used journal in her lap.

The pages still smelled faintly of ink and lavender.

She hadn't written in months—maybe longer. Life had gotten busy. Messy. Uncertain. But something about putting pen to paper now felt necessary. Urgent. Like she needed to hear herself again, without Jayden's voice in the background, without Zara's truth ringing in her ears.

Just her.

She opened to a blank page, took a breath, and began:

"I think I'm falling apart in pieces too small to notice."

The words poured out.

She wrote about the first time she met Jayden, about how he made her feel seen. About the nights he held her like she was everything, and the days he made her feel like nothing. She wrote about the lipstick. The apologies. The soft kisses that quieted her doubts but never answered her questions.

She wrote about how she wanted to believe people could change. That love could be enough.

And then she paused. Pressed the pen against the page. And wrote:

"What if I'm not in love with him? What if I'm in love with the version of him I created in my head?"

The room was silent. No music. No phone buzz. Just the sound of her breathing and the scratch of her pen on paper.

She kept writing—page after page. About fear. About loneliness. About how she missed herself.

And somewhere between the words and the tears, Amara realized something:

She had been giving pieces of herself away, hoping someone else would make her feel whole.

But now, in the quiet, in the truth, she began to see:

The healing wouldn't start with Jayden. It had to start with her.

Amara meets Malik at a business networking event. He's warm, clear about what he wants, and curious about her.

Chapter 7

Enter Malik

Amara almost didn't go.

The business networking event was something her team signed her up for—part of a corporate leadership program she had been too emotionally drained to care about. But Zara had insisted.

"Go," she said. "Dress up. Drink wine. Shake hands. Maybe even meet someone who knows how to communicate in full sentences."

So Amara went.

It was held at a downtown hotel in a glossy rooftop hall overlooking the city skyline. Professionals in tailored suits and polished shoes floated from group to group, armed with name tags and LinkedIn-ready smiles.

Amara stood near the hors d'oeuvres table, pretending to check her phone, silently counting the minutes until it was polite enough to leave.

That's when she heard a voice beside her.

"You look like you're either composing an exit plan or calculating how many spring rolls it'll take to make this night worth it."

She looked up and laughed.

The man beside her had a calm, disarming presence. Clean-shaven, dark suit, subtle cologne. But it was his eyes that held her—curious, steady, and kind.

"A little of both," she replied.

"I'm Malik," he said, extending a hand.

"Amara."

His handshake was firm, but gentle. His smile didn't feel rehearsed. They started talking—first about work. He was an operations strategist for a tech firm. Nothing flashy, but he spoke about it with purpose. Clear. Confident. Grounded.

Unlike Jayden, Malik didn't dodge questions or answer in riddles. He asked about her passions, not just her position. He listened—really listened—when she spoke about the branding campaigns she was proud of.

"You light up when you talk about storytelling," he noted. "That's rare in rooms like this."

Amara blushed slightly, caught off guard.

They moved from the snacks table to a quiet corner with two bar stools. Their conversation drifted naturally—from business to books, from family to future dreams.

And then Malik said something that made her still.

"I don't believe in playing games with people's hearts. Life's too short for confusion. If I like someone, I say it. If I want something, I show up for it."

He didn't say it to impress her. He said it like truth—casual, but unwavering.

Amara smiled, but inside, her heart ached.

Not because Malik had done anything wrong—but because it was the first time in a long time she realized what it felt like to be seen without having to shrink.

He didn't ask for her number that night. He asked if she'd like to meet for coffee sometime—no pressure, no pretending.

And for the first time in months, Amara felt a sense of clarity.

Maybe not about Malik.But about herself.

And what she was starting to believe she deserved.

Jayden notices and becomes distant, then clingy.

Amara hadn't told Jayden about Malik.Not because she was hiding anything—but because there wasn't anything to hide. Not yet. It had just been coffee, conversation, and a quiet realization that not all men made love feel like confusion.

But Jayden noticed.

It started with subtle shifts—small, almost imperceptible. He took longer to reply to her messages. Canceled dinner one evening with a vague excuse about being "swamped." His usual warmth cooled into short, one-word texts and rushed calls that ended before she had a chance to say what was on her mind.

At first, Amara assumed he was just busy again.

But then, the questions started.

"You've been kind of distant lately. Everything good?" "Who were you with yesterday?" "You didn't tell me you had a networking event. Why not?"

She blinked at the sudden interest.Jayden had never been the type to ask. Now he was keeping tabs—half-concerned, half-suspicious.

"You're acting like we're something we've never officially been," Amara finally said, tired.

Jayden didn't respond to that. Instead, the next morning, he showed up at her door with breakfast and a bouquet of tulips—her favorite.

"Thought I'd surprise you," he said with a crooked smile.

He kissed her on the cheek, acted like nothing had changed, and curled up next to her on the couch like he hadn't been emotionally MIA for a week.

It was his pattern—vanish, return, reset. Only this time, it felt like he was holding her tighter. Not out of affection. Out of fear.

Fear that she might finally be slipping from his grip.

He began sending good morning texts again. Calling her at night just to "hear her voice." Suggesting random plans for the weekend.

Talking vaguely about *"getting more serious soon."*

But the words felt rushed.Unstable.As if he was trying to seal cracks in a foundation that had already shifted.

And Amara, now journaling daily, now meeting someone who saw her clearly, began to notice what she once ignored.

Jayden wasn't becoming more present because he wanted to grow.He was becoming more present because he could feel her detaching.

And that terrified him more than losing her had ever done.

Chapter 8

The Big Question

It was a quiet Sunday night.

The kind of night where the world slows down just enough to make you listen to your thoughts. Jayden had cooked—well, tried to. The pasta was a little too salty, the sauce a bit too watery, but Amara smiled through it. Because, for once, he was trying.

They sat on the balcony of his apartment, city lights flickering like distant fireflies. Jayden had poured two glasses of wine and was leaning back in his chair, legs stretched out, face relaxed.

But Amara wasn't relaxed.

Not tonight.

The question had been growing in her for weeks—festering beneath every kiss, every half-truth, every breadcrumb of affection. She needed clarity, not comfort.

So she asked.

"Jayden… what are we doing?"

He didn't answer right away.

He took a sip of wine. Exhaled. Looked out into the distance like he was searching for words he'd buried long ago.

"Why now?" he asked quietly.

"Because I'm tired," she replied. "Tired of wondering. Tired of pretending I don't want more."

Jayden turned to face her fully.

"You know I care about you, Amara."

She nodded slowly. "But is that all it is?"

He leaned forward, elbows resting on his knees. His tone softened.

"You mean a lot to me. I've never connected with someone like this before. You get me. You really *see* me. And that scares the hell out of me sometimes."

Amara's heart thudded.

"Then why can't you say it? Why can't you just... call this what it is?"

Jayden rubbed his hands together, his jaw tightening.

"Because labels mess things up. I've seen it too many times—once people start defining things, it all changes. Expectations rise, pressure builds, and the next thing you know, something real becomes a performance."

"So what do you want?" she asked softly.

"I want *this*," he said, motioning between them. "Us. As we are."

Amara stared at him. He meant it. In his way, he meant every word. But she realised something then—what he wanted wasn't *them*. It was *her presence,* without her expectations.

"You want the warmth of a relationship without the responsibility of one," she said, almost to herself.

Jayden looked away.

Silence stretched between them, wide and unforgiving.

She didn't cry. She didn't yell.She just stood up slowly, placed her glass on the table, and whispered:

"I don't want to be loved in fragments anymore."

And then she walked inside, leaving him out on the balcony—alone with the truth he was too afraid to name.

She lay awake that night, staring at the ceiling of her apartment, the dim light from the hallway casting soft shadows across the walls.

Her body was still, but her mind was at war.

Jayden's words kept echoing in her head: *"I want this. Us. As we are."*

As we are? What were they, really?

A habit. A comfort. A beautiful limbo dressed in the illusion of love. But was it enough?

She missed him the moment she left, and that scared her. Not because she was still in love, but because part of her didn't know how to exist without the longing. The late-night texts. The hopeful waiting. The constant chase of "maybe."

Jayden had become her rhythm. Not always steady.Not always kind.But familiar.

And now, standing on the edge of something better, she felt... lost.

Malik had reached out again that day—just a simple check-in.

*"Hope your weekend's been peaceful."*No pressure. No expectations.

And it struck her how easy it felt. How warm. How safe. But safe was unfamiliar.

She closed her journal after writing just one line:

"How do you walk away from someone you once begged to stay?"

It wasn't about love anymore. It was about *letting go of the version of herself* that believed she wasn't worthy of more than pieces.

She could stay. Fall back into Jayden's arms. Pretend that his caring was enough. But healing meant choosing herself—even if it meant sitting in the loneliness for a while.

Torn between the gravity of habit and the ache of healing, Amara whispered into the silence:

"I want more. Even if it hurts to reach for it."

Chapter 9

Clarity Comes in Silence

For the first time in a long time, Amara didn't answer when Jayden texted.

She didn't block him. Didn't lash out. She left the message unread.

"Thinking of you." A sentence she used to hold onto like a lifeline. Now, it felt like a leash.

She took a few days off work, not because she was falling apart, but because she wanted to be alone with herself, intentionally. Not distracted. Not rushed. Just still.

She woke up late, stayed in pyjamas until noon, and brewed tea instead of coffee. The quiet in her apartment no longer felt empty. It felt sacred.

She journaled every morning. Walked without music. Read books that weren't about love or heartbreak but about self-trust, boundaries, and peace. She cooked simple meals, lit candles, and spoke affirmations into her mirror, not because she believed them yet, but because she wanted to.

"I am enough, even when I am alone." "Love doesn't have to hurt to be real."

There were moments she missed him—sharp, sudden flashes of memory. His laugh, his lazy kisses, the way he used to trace circles on her back while she talked. But each time the nostalgia rose, so did her clarity.

Jayden never made her feel chosen.He made her feel *almost.*

And she was done living in almosts.

In the silence, she heard herself more clearly than she had in months.

She wasn't broken.She wasn't too emotional.She wasn't asking for too much.

She was just asking the wrong person to meet her where she already stood.

One evening, as the sun dipped low and bathed her apartment in amber light, she sat by the window with her journal and wrote:

"Healing isn't loud. It doesn't always come with closure or final words. Sometimes it comes in the quiet, when you finally realise you've stopped begging to be loved."

And in that silence, Amara smiled.

Because for the first time, she felt her peace, and she knew she was never going back.

It had been a full week of silence—no calls from Jayden, no coffee dates, no noise. Just Amara and the quiet hum of her healing.

Then one morning, her doorbell rang.

She padded to the front door in her robe, expecting a delivery she hadn't ordered. When she opened it, there it was—a small bouquet of white lilies and sunflowers, neatly arranged in a simple glass jar. Not showy. Not loud. Just... thoughtful.

Tucked between the petals was an envelope.

Her name, written in smooth, careful handwriting: *Amara.*

She opened it slowly and began to read:

Dear Amara,

I know silence can be beautiful.I also know it can be lonely.

I don't want to crowd your space or rush your process, but I wanted you to know—being around you these past few weeks reminded me of something rare. You speak with kindness even when you're hurting. You listen with your eyes. You smile like it's a choice you make for others, not just yourself.

That's not common.

If you're open to it, I'd love to sit with you again—no expectations.

Just presence.

Warmly, **Malik**

Amara stood there for a long moment, fingers brushing the edge of the note.

He hadn't texted. He hadn't called.He had *written*—with his hands, his heart, and his attention.

And in that moment, something within her stirred.

It wasn't about the flowers.It was the *intention.*

The thoughtfulness.The respect.The emotional clarity she hadn't realized she'd been starving for.

Jayden made her feel like a mystery.Malik made her feel like a masterpiece—one worth seeing clearly.

As she placed the letter beside her journal and brought the flowers into the kitchen, Amara smiled—not because she was ready to love again, but because now she knew exactly what love should feel like.

Chapter 10

The Confrontation

Jayden showed up unannounced.

It was a Thursday evening, just after sunset, when Amara heard the knock. Her chest tightened before she even reached the door.

Something in her already knew—it was time.

She opened it slowly.

There he was. Same eyes. Same quiet presence. But tonight, he looked different. Tense. Like a man bracing for impact.

"I've been calling," he said.

"I know."

"You've been quiet."

"I needed to be."

He shifted on his feet, glanced past her like he was searching for the version of her that used to fold so easily under his charm.

"Can I come in?"

She stepped aside. Not because she owed him anything, but because she deserved closure.

They sat across from each other, silence stretching between them like a final curtain. He spoke first.

"I've been thinking... about everything. About us."

Amara folded her arms, calm but resolved.

"Jayden, there is no 'us.' Not anymore."

His jaw tightened.

"Don't say that. You know what we have is real. I care about you, Amara. Deeply. I just—I'm not wired the way you want me to be."

"I'm not asking you to be anyone else," she said softly. "I'm just tired of shrinking myself to fit inside your comfort zone."

He stood and began pacing, agitated.

"Why can't we just go back to how it was? No pressure. No labels. Just... you and me. The way it felt in the beginning."

Amara stood too. Slowly. Calmly.

"Because that version of 'us' hurt me more than you'll ever understand. I gave you so much of me while begging for a title you knew I deserved. And you fed me just enough affection to keep me hoping."

He stopped pacing. His face cracked—not in anger, but desperation.

"Don't go. Please. Even if we're not official. I just... I need you in my life."

She looked at him then. Really looked.

This was the moment. The test. The same script they'd danced through a dozen times. But this time, she knew the difference: she wasn't confused anymore.

"You don't need *me.* You need access to me. There's a difference."

His eyes glossed over, but he said nothing.

Amara picked up her bag. Walked toward the door. Her hand rested on the handle as she turned back one last time.

"You had all of me, Jayden. And still... it wasn't enough for you to choose me."

And with that, she walked out.

No tears.No dramatic pause.Just peace.

Because this time, she wasn't walking away for attention.

She was walking away for herself.

Jayden didn't follow her.

Not this time.

He just stood there—silent, still—as the door clicked shut behind her. And Amara... didn't look back.

The cool night air wrapped around her like a quiet embrace as she stepped onto the sidewalk. For a moment, she just stood there, letting it sink in. The weight she had carried—the hope, the hurt, the constant wondering—felt lighter with every step she took.

She didn't rush. She didn't run.

She walked.

Past the memories.Past the "almosts."Past the lies she told herself just to hold on.

This time, it wasn't a dramatic exit designed to test his reaction.It wasn't a silence meant to draw him back in.

This was her choosing herself.Finally. Firmly. Freely.

No more waiting for calls.No more reading into half-hearted gestures.No more bending her heart to fit a space he refused to fill.

She didn't know what tomorrow would look like. Whether Malik would become something real or just a gentle reminder that good still existed. She didn't need to know.

All she knew was—she had walked away.

For real.

For herself.

Chapter 11

Healing & Hope

The days that followed weren't perfect.Healing rarely is.

There were mornings Amara woke up missing Jayden's voice, and nights she reached for her phone out of habit before pulling her hand back. But something had changed—not just around her, but *within* her.

She had finally stopped romanticising his potential and started prioritizing her peace.

She signed up for therapy that week.

Not because she was broken, but because she wanted to understand herself better. The patterns she repeated. The wounds she'd covered with pretty words. The reason she kept choosing men who made her feel like she had to earn love.

Her therapist, a soft-spoken woman with sharp insight, didn't rush her healing.She listened. Challenged. Affirmed.

"You can be deeply empathetic," she once said, "and still have boundaries. You can love someone and still walk away if they cannot meet you where you are."

Amara carried those words like armor.

She also poured herself into her writing again.

What started as late-night journal entries turned into essays—then stories. Reflections on heartbreak, boundaries, and rediscovery. Her pain had become her power. And with every word she wrote, she reclaimed a little more of herself.

She lit candles in the evenings. Played music that soothed her soul. Took herself out to brunch. Bought flowers for her own table. Read books that reminded her of her worth.

And slowly, she began to smile again—not because of someone else, but because of how deeply she was beginning to love her own company.

Malik messaged her every now and then—kind, respectful, never pushy.

And while part of her was curious, she wasn't rushing into anything. She was finally building something with herself. Something solid. Something whole.

Healing wasn't loud or dramatic.It came in quiet moments.In honest conversations.In learning to say "no" without guilt.In waking up and realizing she hadn't thought about Jayden at all.

Amara had given so much of herself to people who didn't know how to hold her.

Now, she was learning to hold herself.

And for the first time in a long time, *that* was enough.

Epilogue

One year later.

The café buzzed with soft chatter, the smell of roasted coffee beans swirling through the air. Amara sat by the window, sunlight spilling across her journal and a newly printed proof copy of her first book.

Title: *"The Situationship Dilemma: Lessons in Loving Myself First."*

Her name on the cover made her smile—not out of vanity, but quiet pride. She had bled on the page. Told the truth. Pulled her heart out and shaped it into something others could hold.

What started as private journal entries in a dimly lit apartment had become essays, reflections, and hard-won wisdom about modern love—its illusions, its traps, and its possibilities. It wasn't a book about heartbreak. It was about clarity. Boundaries. Choosing self-worth in a world that romanticized confusion.

She had just left a radio interview where she spoke about her journey, her healing, and why she believed love without clarity was emotional debt no one should pay.

"We don't talk enough about what it means to unlearn struggle as a love language," she'd said into the mic. "I wrote this book to remind people—especially women—that love isn't supposed to hurt to be real. And you don't have to stay in almost-relationships to prove your worth."

Her phone buzzed. A message from Malik.

"Saw the interview. You were brilliant. Dinner to celebrate?"

Amara smiled.

They'd kept in touch, slowly, softly. He never pushed. Never rushed. Just showed up—in kindness, in conversation, in consistency. They had gone on a few dates. Nothing heavy. Nothing forced. Just mutual respect and ease. The way she now believed love should start.

She looked out the window. The city was still noisy. Still unpredictable. But she was steady now. Grounded.

No more waiting to be chosen.No more shrinking to fit someone else's "almost."She had written her way back to herself.

And in doing so, she discovered the kind of love she had once begged for—

Her own.

She arrived at the restaurant just after sunset. Malik was already there, waiting with his usual quiet smile and a seat pulled out just for her. He stood as she approached—simple gestures, nothing performative. Just respect. Presence.

"Congratulations, author," he said, handing her a small envelope. Inside was a handwritten note:

"For choosing yourself first. That's where real love begins."

Amara looked up at him, her heart full—but not desperate. Not anxious.Steady.

Their relationship had blossomed slowly, deliberately. There were no blurred lines, no late-night guessing games, no emotional gymnastics. Malik was patient. Intentional. Honest. And most importantly—he never asked her to become less of herself to be loved.

They weren't defining forever. They were living fully in now.

But this time, it was *her* now.

A now she entered on her own terms.

She no longer felt the need to chase love or shrink to be chosen.She didn't fear being alone—because she had learned how to be whole.And standing beside someone like Malik, she finally realized—

Love isn't about losing yourself to be accepted.It's about *knowing yourself so well* that no one else gets to decide your worth.

As they clinked glasses to celebrate the launch of her book, Amara smiled—not because she had found the right man, but because she had finally become the right woman for herself.

She knew what she deserved.

And she'd never settle for less again.

www.ingramcontent.com/pod-product-compliance
Lightning Source LLC
Chambersburg PA
CBHW071317200626
46813CB00015B/2247